The Little Fir Tree

Christopher Corr

From an original story
by Hans Christian Andersen

chartwell
books

Deep in the forest,
there lived a beautiful little fir tree.
The sun shone warmly, the birds sang and a cool breeze blew,
but the little fir tree was unhappy.

"When will I be big and tall like the other trees?" he wondered.
"Then the birds would build their nests in my branches and sing to me.
Now I am so small that no one pays me any attention."

Suddenly, a hare leapt over the little fir tree
and he felt smaller than ever.

Soon it was summertime and children came with baskets of berries.
They sat next to the fir tree as they ate their fruit.

"What a perfect little tree," they said, stroking his branches.
"He is so pretty and sweet."

The little fir tree sighed. "I don't want to be pretty and sweet,"
he thought. "And I wish they'd leave my branches alone."

Then autumn came
and the lumberjacks arrived with saws and axes.
Some of the giant trees crashed to the floor and the ground shook!

"Where are you going?" the little fir tree asked the giant trees.
"Can I come too?"

But the giant trees didn't reply.

"Don't worry," said Squirrel, as the little fir tree fretted.
"It will be your turn one day."

The next morning the birds arrived.

"What happened to the trees that got taken away?"
asked the little fir tree.

"They have become cabins for people to live inside,
standing sturdy and strong on the edge of the forest," said the birds.

"I wish I was bigger so I could be a cabin,"
said the little fir tree.

He was so busy imagining it that he didn't notice
the butterflies fluttering around him.

"Oh, I wish I could become a ship and sail on the sea,"
said the little fir tree. "What is the sea?"

The birds laughed.
"Don't wish your life away, little tree.
Every moment is precious.
Look at the sunlight falling
through the green leaves.
It's so beautiful."

But the little fir tree wasn't listening.

The seasons came and went.

Two whole years passed and the little fir tree grew taller.
When people came by they said,

"What a fine-looking tree!"

"What a wonderful tree!"

Then it was winter.
The snow fell and a cold wind blew from the north.

The lumberjacks arrived and this time the
little fir tree was the first to be cut down.
"Finally, I will see the world!" he thought, his heart soaring.

The little fir tree was loaded onto a cart and wheeled into town.

Then he was carried up into a grand house
and placed in a beautiful room.

Some children began to hang tinsel,
baubles and ribbons
on his branches.

They lit candles and finally
tied a gold star to the very top of him.

"He is such a beautiful tree,
so handsome and so tall," they said,
clapping their hands in delight.

"I wish my old friends the squirrel and the birds
could see me now," thought the little fir tree proudly.

In the evening the room filled with lots of people.
When they saw the little fir tree covered in
candles and sweeties and baubles,
they danced around him with joy.

"Now it is time for a story," said the father.
"I will tell you the tale of The Snow Queen.
It is about two dear friends Gerda and Kai, and how Gerda
risks her life to look for Kai when he is taken away
to Lapland in the frozen north."

The little fir tree listened attentively,
for he had never heard a story before.

When the story was finished,
the little fir tree was once again surrounded by people.
They ate all the sweeties and untied all the ribbons
until he looked like a forest tree again.

Later, when everyone had gone to bed,
the little fir tree thought about everything that had happened.
"I can't wait for it to begin again.
Perhaps I will get different ribbons tomorrow!"

But the next day,
two men carried the little fir tree
out of the room

and out of the house
to the shed.

They closed the door, leaving him in the dark.

Hours went by, and no one came.

"What is happening now?"
thought the little fir tree.
"This isn't what I thought the
world would be like."

To pass the time, the little fir tree thought of the woods.
He remembered the feel of the warm sun
and the fresh breeze on his leaves.

He thought of how the animals were so kind to him,
and the birds too. He even missed the big hare.

"It was the best place in the world," he thought.
"If only I'd known it then."

When spring came,
so did an old friend.

"Hello little fir tree,"
said Squirrel. "How did you come
to be here, and what have you seen
of the world
since we last met?"

The little fir tree told him of the wonderful candles and baubles
and the story of the Snow Queen and Kai and Gerda.
"It was beautiful," he said, "but not as beautiful as the forest."
And the little fir tree sighed sadly.

The squirrel squeaked in reply, so loudly
that the children heard. They opened the door of the shed
to see what was making the noise.

"It's our old tree!" they said excitedly,
and they dragged the little fir tree outside.

The children decorated the little fir tree again,
but this time with flowers and leaves.

He breathed in the fresh air as he heard the laughter of the children.
"This is the place for me," he thought.
As the sun warmed his branches and the breeze tickled his leaves,
for the first time, the little fir tree was happy.

Midsummer arrived
and the sun was hot
and high in the sky.

The birds swooped
and dived as butterflies caressed
the perfumed flowers and bees buzzed
as they fed from the blossoms.

And out of the ground,
where the squirrel kept his larder…

there grew a new beautiful little fir tree.